Walt Disney's
DUMBO
FAVORITES

DUMBO
FAVORITES

THE DANBURY PRESS

THE DANBURY PRESS
a division of Grolier Enterprises Inc.

Robert B. Clarke   *Publisher*

The Stonehouse Press   *Production Supervision*

ISBN 0–71–72–8110–8

Printed and bound in Great Britain by
Morrison & Gibb Ltd., London and Edinburgh

234567899876 5

Introduction

Dumbo was almost a failure. When the other elephants saw his big ears, they laughed. It took a little mouse named Timothy to give Dumbo confidence and teach him to flap those big ears and fly.

After that Dumbo became the star of the circus. He had many wonderful adventures, and some of his favorites are included in this book. Maybe as you read you can imagine yourself at a circus, with the smell of freshly roasted popcorn, the merry sounds of the band, the dry crunch of the sawdust and . . . But turn the page and begin having fun!

Table of Contents

TITLE   PAGE

Mrs. Jumbo's Baby   10

The Scarecrow Caper   18

Dumbo Finds Bertie   24

Jungle Train   32

Hide-and-Seek   40

Bongo's Birthday Cake   46

The Snake Charmer   52

Jungle Jogging   58

Crazy, Mixed-up Car   66

A Howling Success   72

A Day at the Carnival   74

Bongo Takes a Trip   82

After the Hats   90

Mickey and the Big Brown Bear   96

"Let 'Em Eat Cake"   98

Bongo's Good Deed   110

Pasting a Clown   116

TITLE	PAGE
Boys and Gulls	124
Mickey and the Chewed Shoes	132
Jungle Sports	134
It's Done with Mirrors	140
Bone Burying	148
The Train in Spain	150
Up, Up and Away	158
The Great Ravioli	164
High Wire Herman	172
Dumbo Helps Out	178

Mrs. Jumbo's Baby

When Mrs. Jumbo had her baby, everybody in the circus was very excited. It had been years since an elephant had been born, and the whole circus family was eager to see what its newest member looked like. The clowns, tumblers, trapeze artists — in fact, everybody — rushed to the elephant tent. There they waited until Mrs. Jumbo pushed her baby gently outside.

"Why, it's a boy," shouted a clown.

"It has blue eyes," said the lion tamer.

The baby raised his head and tried to flap his ears. There was a gasp from the circus people.

"Why, he has the biggest ears I've ever seen!" said Mr. Ringmaster.

It was true. Mrs. Jumbo's baby had the biggest ears of any elephant in the world. They looked like enormous wings when they were stretched out.

The circus family was proud to have a baby elephant with such cute ears.

The other elephants, however, poked fun at Mrs. Jumbo and her baby.

"Why call him Jumbo?" snorted a big elephant. "He looks so stupid with those big ears, you ought to call him Dumbo."

The other elephants roared with laughter. Mrs. Jumbo tried to make them stop, but they wouldn't.

At that moment a little circus mouse named Timothy heard the uproar and crawled into the tent. He declared, "Those big blimps are teasing Mrs. Jumbo. I'll put a stop to that!"

The mouse ran up to them, stood on his hind legs and shouted, "Boo!" The elephants, who were afraid of mice, all ran away.

Timothy chuckled and looked around for the baby. He found him hiding under a pile of hay. "You don't have to be afraid of me," squeaked Timothy. "I want to be your friend. Uh, er — what did you say your name was?"

"I think it's Dumbo," the little elephant answered.

"Okay, Dumbo,
I'm Timothy,"
said the mouse.
"Hi, Timothy,"
said Dumbo.
Within minutes
they were friends.
Dumbo was happy.
"Now I have
a real friend,"
he smiled.

When he was older, Dumbo wanted to join the elephant act, but he was too awkward. He kept tripping over his ears. This made him unhappy because he wanted to be an important part of circus life.

"What am I going to do?" he moaned one day to Timothy. "The other elephants don't want me in their act."

"Get your own act!" said Timothy.

Timothy taught Dumbo to fly by using his big ears. Almost overnight Dumbo became a star, and people came from everywhere to see him fly around the circus tent. Now Dumbo was a star, and nobody teased him about his ears.

Mr. Ringmaster had double reason to appreciate Dumbo. One day Dumbo was near Mr. Ringmaster's trailer when it caught fire.

"Quick, Dumbo," squeaked Timothy. "You've got to put the fire out. Stick your trunk in this bucket of water."

Dumbo did as he was told.

He sucked up all the water. Then, with Timothy in his hat, he flew to the trailer and squirted water at the flames. Soon the fire was out.

"Hooray!" yelled Mr. Ringmaster. "You saved my home."

As a thank you, he gave Dumbo some extra goodies that night for dinner.

The Scarecrow Caper

One day Dumbo and Timothy Mouse decided to visit their old friends the crows. These feathered fellows were usually happy and full of fun, but this afternoon they were sad and glum.

"What's the matter?" asked Dumbo. "We came to have fun, and what do we find? Four sad-faced birds who look as though they've lost their best friend."

"We *have* lost our best friend," said one crow. "Our favorite scarecrow is gone."

"What happened?" asked Timothy.

"Two boys came along, stole the scarecrow and threw it into a ditch," said the crow. "And sitting on a hard wooden fence isn't nearly as comfortable as sitting on the arms of that old scarecrow."

"If you promise to cheer up," Dumbo said, "I'll get your scarecrow back for you."

"Hooray!" they shouted.

Dumbo found the scarecrow, which was covered with mud from the ditch.

The third crow said, "We can't sit on that. We'll get all dirty."

"Okay. We'll take care of that, too," said Timothy. "See that water over there, Dumbo? Use your trunk to hose off the dirty scarecrow and get things back to normal."

While Dumbo was slurping up the water, on the other side of a large hedge were Tom and Ted, the two boys who had thrown the scarecrow into the mud.

Tom yelled, "Look! The farmer has put his scarecrow up again. Let's throw it back in the ditch."

As they scrambled over the hedge, Dumbo raised his trunk and squirted water at the scarecrow. SWOOSH! It sprayed the boys, too.

Tom wailed, "I'm all wet! Where did the water come from?"

The two boys
couldn't see Dumbo
on the other side
of the hedge.

Dumbo whispered to Timothy, "We'll give them a scare they won't forget." He picked up the scarecrow and started moving toward Tom and Ted.

"Boo!" shouted Timothy. "Boo!"

The boys thought the scarecrow was alive and after them! "Help!" they screamed. "It's coming after us." Their eyes wide with fright, they ran away.

The crows laughed and laughed. "Serves you right," they called.

"It'll be a long time before they come back here again," said the first crow.

The third crow laughed,
"You certainly scared them
with that scarecrow, Dumbo.
That's the funniest thing
I've seen in ages."
Dumbo laughed, too.

Dumbo put the scarecrow back in the field and said goodbye to his friends. "Time for us to get back to the circus!"

"Come back soon," called the crows, perching comfortably on the scarecrow.

Dumbo Finds Bertie

Pah! Pah! Ooom-pah-pah!

Ta-ta-ta, dee-doo-day!

Sally's Performing Seals were rehearsing "The Elephant Lullaby," Dumbo's favorite song. As always, Dumbo and Timothy Mouse were nearby, watching and listening.

"Isn't that a wonderful song?" said Dumbo gleefully. "It sure has rhythm," answered Timothy, snapping his fingers.

Suddenly the rehearsal stopped. Sally walked over to Bertie, the baby seal who played the tuba. He said, "I'm not going to play the tuba any more. It's too hard to blow and I'm tired!"

Sally replied, "Then there'll be no fish for you when we're finished!"

"I don't care. I know where there are lots of fish to eat. I think I'll get some." With that, Bertie headed for the main gate.

That night, when the show was about to begin, Sally discovered that Bertie was missing. All the circus performers helped search for him, but they couldn't find him anywhere.

"Where can Bertie be?" Dumbo asked Timothy. "I'm worried about him because I like him. Besides, he's my favorite tuba player."

Timothy scratched his head.

The mouse said,
"Remember when
he said he was going
to where there were
lots of fish?
Well, that could
only be the ocean!"
"You're right,"
cried Dumbo.

Timothy jumped
into Dumbo's hat
and off they flew
for the beach.
It was getting dark.

They passed over the city with its
bright lights and finally landed on a
long, sandy beach.

Suddenly Timothy shouted, "I think I see Bertie. He's sitting on a rock down there."

"Hold on tight. I'm going to nose-dive," Dumbo said. He flipped his ears, and down they sped. They landed next to Bertie on the rock.

Poor Bertie. He was crying. "All the fish have gone to bed," he sobbed. "I've been searching for a fish to eat for hours, and I haven't found a single one. I'm cold and hungry."

"You've been a silly seal," said Dumbo. "Now let us take you home."

Dumbo arrived at the circus just as Sally was leading her seals into the circus tent. Dumbo said to Bertie, "Go on in there and play 'The Elephant Lullaby' like only you can play it."

Bertie was glad to be back at the circus. He gave Sally a big kiss, and she gave him all the fish he wanted.

Dumbo's Friends

Dumbo was a circus elephant, and since people in show business usually stick together, it seemed only natural that he made friends with Bongo the bear and Mowgli.

Bongo, a fugitive from a circus, liked to ride around on his one-wheel cycle. He couldn't go as fast as a flying elephant, but he could make that cycle hum. At times it seemed as if Bongo could do more with his cycle on the ground than Dumbo could flying in the air.

Mowgli was another of Dumbo's pals. Mowgli's closest buddies were Baloo the bear, Bagheera the panther, and Colonel Hathi the elephant. The colonel's little son was a special favorite of both Dumbo and Mowgli. He looked a lot like Dumbo but because of his small ears, he was in the infantry, not the air force.

The jungle friends never performed in a circus the way Dumbo did, but Dumbo would often fly to the jungle and visit. He would spend the evening telling them about the circus, and they would tell him about the jungle.

Some of the best adventures of Bongo and Mowgli are on the following pages. Dumbo hopes that everyone will enjoy reading about them — and also about his old friend, Mickey Mouse.

Jungle Train

One day Mowgli and Baloo noticed some strange puffs of smoke in the distant sky. They climbed a tree to see where the smoke was coming from. As they stared, puzzled, a buzzard sat down beside them and said that the smoke came from a train.

Mowgli had heard of trains but had never seen one. "Come on, Baloo," he said.

"Naw. Trains give me pains," Baloo answered. But Mowgli insisted, so off they went to investigate the train.

They came to the railroad track, and there stood the engine, all black and shiny with bright brass trimmings. It gave off smoke and soft hissing noises.

"Sounds like Kaa the python,"
Mowgli remarked to Baloo.
"Let's get a closer look."
But Baloo hesitated.

Old Baloo
wasn't sure
he liked
anything
that sounded
like Kaa,
but he
moved forward
with Mowgli.

Just then the engine shot out a jet of steam. SWOOSH!

Baloo yelled in fright and galloped into the jungle, with little Mowgli hanging on his shoulders. He almost trampled the engine fireman, who was carrying a load of firewood.

At the sight of the bear the fireman let out a yell, dropped his load of wood and streaked back toward the engine. "Let's get out of here!"

The engineer called back, "We can't move. We haven't enough steam, and we're out of fuel."

The fireman wailed, "What'll we do?"

Mowgli laughed when he heard them shouting. "I think they're more scared of you, Baloo, than you are of their engine!" Baloo laughed, too.

"Scared of me?" Baloo asked. "Don't they know I want to help people, not scare them?"

Mowgli had an idea. "I know how we can un-scare them," he said. He didn't think the engine was dangerous, and he wanted to show the two trainmen that he and Baloo were friendly.

He gathered up all the wood the fireman had dropped. Baloo went into the forest and, using his great strength, uprooted a few old trees. The boy and the big bear carried piles and piles of wood to the engine.

"You don't have to be scared of old Baloo here," Mowgli said to the surprised trainmen.

"This bear's the kindliest and friendliest creature in the whole jungle," Mowgli added. Baloo grinned broadly, nodding in agreement.

The delighted fireman and engineer got up a head of steam, and they asked Mowgli and Baloo if they'd like a ride.

"*Would* we!" they cried together!

They went chuffing and hissing down the track. To Baloo's ears, the hissing didn't sound like Kaa any more — it was friendly hissing. Baloo perched on the stack of firewood in the tender and enjoyed every minute of the trip.

The engineer let Mowgli blow the whistle and ring the bell to let all the jungle-dwellers know that the engine was coming. Baloo loved the sound of the whistle and kept trying to imitate it as he rode along. "Whooo! Whooo!" he called. "Do I sound like an engine, Mowgli? Wait'll old Bagheera hears me."

When their ride was over, Baloo kept going, "Whooo! Whooo!" all the way home. "Hey, Baggy," he yelled at the panther. "We went for a ride on the train. Bet you wish you could have been along. Whooo! Whooo!"

Baloo kept making noises like a whistle the rest of the day. Finally Bagheera had to cover up his ears.

"Aw, you're jealous because you didn't get to go," said Baloo.

The panther moaned, "With you making that noise, Baloo, who *needs* to go on a train ride?"

Hide-and-Seek

Dumbo and Timothy Mouse were playing hide-and-seek. Dumbo shut his eyes and started to count, and Timothy scampered off. Dumbo took three minutes counting to fifty because it was hard to do, and he never peeked once.

Finally he started searching for the mouse. He looked under the lion's cage and in the strong man's tent.

Dumbo thought, "Maybe I should have peeked a little — just enough to see what direction he took." He looked behind the popcorn machine and in the main tent.

He spotted Mr. Ringmaster, who was about to fire a new cannon.

"Hello, Dumbo," shouted Mr. Ringmaster. "Have you come to see if my cannon works?"

"No, sir. I'm looking for Timothy Mouse, and I think he's in here somewhere."

"I hope he's not hiding in my cannon," laughed Mr. Ringmaster.

The fuse spluttered and got shorter and shorter.

BOOM!

Smoke erupted from the mouth of the cannon. Alas, so did Timothy Mouse! He had been hiding in there, and now he was sailing toward the far end of the tent.

Mr. Ringmaster shouted, "What are we going to do? There's no safety net. He's going to land in the wooden seats!"

Dumbo started flapping his ears and took off after his friend. "I'm coming, Timothy. Don't be afraid."

The elephant zoomed toward the mouse, who was beginning to fall toward the ground. Timothy was shouting, "Save me! Save me!"

Dumbo answered, "I'm trying!"

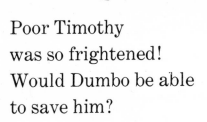

Poor Timothy was so frightened! Would Dumbo be able to save him?

Timothy opened his eyes and saw the seats rushing toward him. That frightened him so much that he shut them again. Tightly. He shouted one last "Help!"

Inches before Timothy was to land, Dumbo reached out with his trunk and caught him. "Boy, that was close," squeaked the mouse.

Mr. Ringmaster applauded Dumbo's performance. "We should put that in your act," he said.

"No way," answered Timothy. "And I'm never, never going to hide in a cannon again. In fact, I may never play hide-and-seek again."

"It was a good place to hide," Dumbo admitted.

Mr. Ringmaster brought them something to eat, and Dumbo laughed, "Our game almost ended with a bang! Instead, it ended with a banana!"

Bongo's Birthday Cake

Bongo was a circus bear who liked to ride a one-wheel cycle. Even when he was not with the circus, Bongo always found that his performing tricks came in handy.

One day he was merrily wheeling down the street when an old lady called to him. She said, "I have baked a birthday cake for my granddaughter. Unhappily I can't deliver it because the rains have made the roads so wet. Could you please take it to her for me? It would make her very happy, I'm sure."

Bongo was only too pleased to help. "Don't worry. I'll see that she gets it in time for her party," he said.

He took the cake, and off he went. The roads were muddy because of the rains.

Cars and trucks whizzed by Bongo, splashing water near the cake. He used all his tricks to keep it dry.

One car spun him around, and the
cake slipped out of his hands. It sailed
through the air toward a big field. Bongo
was so concerned with catching the cake
that he didn't see a bull standing close
by. The bull and the bear both wanted
that cake.

Bongo snatched it from under the
bull's horns. He said, "Bulls aren't supposed to like cake. Grass is much better
for you."

The bull didn't agree.

Horns lowered, the bull snorted and huffed and pawed the ground. Then he took off after the little bear.

The grass was slick, and twice Bongo almost tipped over as he pedaled quickly through the field. Luckily Bongo was good at keeping his balance.

He looked behind him, saw the bull with those big horns and churned his legs even faster. He could feel the bull's breath on his back, and it scared him!

Bongo was so busy
trying to escape
from the bull that
he didn't know
he was heading
for a cliff.

Over the cliff he went.
He flew off into space.
Below he saw some tele-
phone wires. He thought,
"If I can land on one of
those wires, I won't end
up in the river and ruin
the cake." He leaned a
little this way and
pushed a little that way
until he landed smack on
a wire.

Riding on a wire was
easy for the performing
bear. He zipped along.

He pedaled happily along the wire, up and down between the poles, over the river, along the highway, above the flooded fields, until he reached the granddaughter's house. He rang the doorbell and delivered the cake safe and sound.

The little girl invited him inside.

He performed at her party, and the children insisted he have some of the birthday cake. As he ate he said, "A cake in the hand is far better than applause in the ears!"

The Snake Charmer

Dumbo had many friends in the circus, but the one that worried him the most was Cyril the snake. Cyril belonged to Mr. Swami, the snake charmer. Without that funny green snake, Mr. Swami had nothing to do. That was the problem. Cyril kept slithering off somewhere.

One day Dumbo was alarmed to see Cyril crawling away at show time.

"Where are you going?" asked Dumbo.

"I'm jus-s-st s-s-slipping outs-s-ide to s-s-see s-s-somebody," he hissed.

"But your act is on next," Dumbo told him.

"I'll be back in time," Cyril replied as he slithered under the canvas.

Mr. Ringmaster called to Mr. Swami, "Get ready to go on."

"I'm ready," said Mr. Swami, not knowing his snake was gone.

Timothy Mouse spoke up. "Don't worry, Dumbo. I've got an idea. We'll cover for Cyril. Get into the snake's basket."

"Me? How can an elephant take the place of a snake?"

"You'll see," Timothy chuckled as he dipped a brush in some paint.

"Ummph!" grunted Mr. Swami, carrying the basket into the circus ring. "Cyril, you're getting heavier every day."

He put the basket on the carpet and started to play his pipe. Dumbo raised his

trunk, which Timothy had painted to look like Cyril. Dumbo waved it to-and-fro in time to the music. To the audience the trunk looked like Cyril swinging and swaying to the music.

It was a dreamy, enchanting tune. Dumbo was carried away, so much so that he began wiggling his big ears.

Dumbo floated right out of the basket.

"Ooo-o-o," gasped the audience. "Look at that! What a surprise! What a wonderful act!"

Mr. Swami opened his eyes to see what his silly snake was up to. Was he ever surprised to see a floating elephant!

The music
stopped, and
Dumbo woke up
with a start!
He fell,
bump-bump,
on the basket.
The audience
roared
with laughter.

Mr. Swami got angry and began waving his arms and shouting at poor Dumbo. Everyone thought it was part of the act and laughed even louder.

"Wonderful," said Mr. Ringmaster, shaking Mr. Swami's hand. "Dumbo is no substitute for Cyril, but that was the funniest surprise act I've ever seen."

Soon Mr. Swami was chuckling, too. "No wonder the basket was so heavy," he said. He went to Dumbo and said, "Thanks. I don't know where Cyril is, but you saved me!"

"Thank Timothy," Dumbo replied. "It was his idea and his paint. I felt pretty silly looking at my painted trunk and seeing those eyes staring back at me!"

Cyril crawled into the tent. "A very good idea it was-s-s," he said.

Cyril added, "As-s-s s-s-soon as-s-s we get a new bas-s-sket, Dumbo will have to be a s-s-snake again!"

Jungle Jogging

It was early morning in the jungle, and Shere Khan hadn't eaten breakfast yet. He was very hungry. He happened to see Baloo, who was jogging through the jungle singing to himself, "Doobie-doo and a razz-ma-tazz, hey-bob-a-ree-bop and all that jazz!"

Shere Khan made a sour face and put his paws over his ears. Baloo's singing wasn't good, but it was loud.

Baloo loved to sing, but few other animals liked his voice. Yet everyone loved Baloo — except Shere Khan, who didn't love anybody!

Baloo's singing didn't spoil Shere Khan's appetite. "I'll bet Baloo is going to meet the man-cub," the tiger muttered. "I think I'll follow him. He'll lead me right to my breakfast — Mowgli!" The tiger grinned and licked his chops with a loud slurp.

Shere Khan began trotting after Baloo, who danced through the jungle on his tiptoes, happily singing. "I hope he's not going too far," growled the tiger. "I didn't sleep last night and I'm tired."

Baloo danced along until he came to a steep hill. Shere Khan groaned, "Oh no, he's not heading up that mountain!"

Up the hill went Baloo, with the tiger scrambling behind, trying to stay out of sight and puffing with every step. As he skipped along, Baloo chuckled, "This is the best day of the month."

"It'll be *my* best day, too, if I get my claws on Mowgli," Shere Khan grunted.

After a while the tiger wondered, "How much farther is he going? I'm getting more tired with every step!" But if Baloo knew how much farther he had to go, he wasn't saying.

Along the path Baloo was skipping, dancing, jogging, hopping, bobbing, bounding, flouncing and frisking. Shere Khan was staggering.

Shere Khan found it harder and harder to keep up. Not only that, Baloo seemed to choose the most difficult paths to follow. He hopped onto a log to cross a deep, swift river, balancing like a circus star in the center ring. The tiger groaned, "Oh no. Crossing rivers on logs makes me dizzy."

As he hopped along, Baloo sang, "Mowgli sure is going to be ... happy to see little old me."

At the sound of Mowgli's name, Shere Khan's ears perked up. "Ah, so Baloo *is* going to meet the man-cub," he said to himself. "I'd better keep going."

On through the jungle Baloo jogged, mile after mile after mile. Shere Khan's new-found strength soon gave out.

After another five miles, Shere Khan's noble chin was practically dragging on the ground. He peered sleepily after Baloo with half-closed eyes. "I don't think I can go any farther," he yawned. "I'm so-o-o tired."

Suddenly Baloo let out a whoop. "Hiya, Mowgli. How ya doing?"

By now Shere Khan had lost all interest in food. All he wanted to do was sleep.

"Sorry if I kept you waiting, Little Britches," laughed Baloo. "This is the first day of the month, and I always run my twenty miles to keep in shape."

Mowgli said, "I knew this was your day to exercise, so I took my time."

"I've really worked up an appetite," Baloo chuckled. "What do you say to finding some breakfast?"

Off went the two friends, arm in arm. As for Shere Khan, he lay behind a rock and snored. His breakfast would be only in his dreams.

Crazy, Mixed-up Car

Charlie the clown invited Dumbo and Timothy to see the tryout of his new act. Beep! Honk!

"Look, Dumbo," cried Timothy. "Charlie has a brand new car!"

Charlie drove into the ring in the funniest car Dumbo had ever seen. It shook, chugged and rattled.

Charlie sang in a loud voice as he drove the car around and around.

Bang! The hood of Charlie's car flew open, and steam shot out of the engine.

Dumbo shouted, "Something's wrong!"

"Ha, ha! That was supposed to happen," roared Charlie. He pulled a lever, and the trunk fell off. "That's part of the act, too." Then Charlie fell out of the car!

Dumbo and Timothy couldn't stop laughing as Charlie picked himself up and dusted himself off.

"You certainly have a clever car," Dumbo told Charlie. "Now it's driving itself out of the ring!"

"Huh?" gasped Charlie, whirling around. "Hey!" he shouted when he saw the car heading for the main entrance. "You're not supposed to do that. Come back! I've got to stop you before you escape!"

The little car chugged on merrily, right out of the tent!

"Help! Somebody stop my car. It's getting away." The only person who heard Charlie yell was an old clown who was balancing on a ball. He was much too busy to worry about Charlie's car.

"Puff, puff! That car . . . cost me every . . . penny I had. What . . . am I — puff — going to do?" asked Charlie.

The little car went faster. Soon it was far away, and it looked like it was getting completely away.

"I can stop it," cried Dumbo.
"But you . . . don't know what . . .
to — puff — do!" gasped Charlie.

"I do," said Timothy. "Quick, Dumbo,
fly to the car."

Dumbo flapped his ears and was soon
over the car. Timothy pointed to a lever.
"That's the brake. Grab it and pull it."

Unfortunately, Timothy made a terrible mistake. The car didn't stop. Instead,
it fell completely apart. There were pieces
of it everywhere! What a mess!

"I'm sorry," sighed Dumbo.

"I'm sorry, too," said the mouse. "I guess I was looking at the wrong lever. I didn't mean to break the car."

"You didn't break it," laughed Charlie. "It's supposed to fall apart. It's a crazy circus car."

"It is?" said Dumbo. He was feeling better now.

Charlie quickly put the car together. Dumbo was amazed. "Now I'll take you for a ride," said Charlie. "I promise it won't break." And it didn't.

A Howling Success

Mickey Mouse had a new job. He was a house-watcher. He stayed in a house while the owners took a restful vacation to Tierra del Fuego. To keep him company, Mickey brought Pluto along.

For a while everything went fine, but after seven days there was a full moon.

"AAAooooOOOO!"

Mickey grabbed a flashlight and went outside. He thought Pluto had the world's worst stomach ache. But Pluto wasn't sick. He was baying at the moon.

Clarabelle Cow, who lived across the street, opened her window and yelled, "Is anybody sick? Should I call an ambulance?"

Mickey got everybody settled down and went back to sleep.

The next night it happened again.

"AAAooooOOOO!"

Mickey rushed downstairs to soothe Pluto. Clarabelle Cow opened her window again and yelled, "Who's sick? Should I call an ambulance?"

Mickey calmed everybody and went back to bed. The next night, there it was again.

"AAAoooOOOO!"

Mickey ran downstairs — smack into a burglar who was stealing the silverware. Clarabelle yelled, "Should I call an ambulance?" Mickey replied, "No, get a policeman."

The police arrived and took the burglar to jail. There was a reward, which Mickey shared with Pluto.

"After all," he explained, "if Pluto hadn't howled I'd never have been awake to catch the burglar!"

A Day at
the Carnival

It was a quiet evening at the circus grounds. There was no show in the Big Top, and Dumbo had nothing to do. He gazed longingly at the carnival across the field. The bright lights and sounds of fun were exciting to the little elephant.

"Everyone seems so happy over there," Dumbo said to Timothy Mouse. "It must be lots of fun. Let's see for ourselves."

"It's very late," answered Timothy, "and there are so many people over there, we might get trampled." But Dumbo was already on his way to the carnival.

The elephant and mouse landed behind one of the show tents. "Hear all that shouting?" said Dumbo. "What's happening?"

As they rounded the corner of the tent somebody threw a wooden ball at a target. SWISHHH! It missed the target and knocked off Dumbo's hat, almost hitting him on the head. "Whew!" said Dumbo.

"Maybe you were right, Timothy. Let's come back tomorrow."

Next morning, Dumbo and Timothy returned to the carnival, but it wasn't at all the same. The side shows and booths were closed.

It was very quiet, and nobody was around except old Mr. Donk, the owner of the merry-go-round. "Maybe he will give us a ride," said Timothy.

"I'm very sorry," said Mr. Donk. "I would gladly give you a ride, but the merry-go-round is broken and won't go around."

"Perhaps it's stuck," Timothy suggested. "If you pushed and Dumbo pulled, it might get unstuck."

Mr. Donk thought that was a good idea. He pushed and Dumbo pulled. CLUNK-bzzz-KER-CHUNK!

With a jolt the merry-go-round started. It whizzed around so fast that Dumbo was knocked down and Mr. Donk was whipped off his feet and whizzed around with it.

"Help! Stop it!" he cried.

"I must save him.
He might get hurt!"
shouted Dumbo.
Flapping his ears,
Dumbo grabbed
a whizzing bar
with his trunk.

Dumbo flapped his ears, pulling in the opposite direction. Gradually the merry-go-round slowed down and then stopped. A dizzy Mr. Donk stepped on solid ground.

"Phew!" he gasped.
"I don't want
any more of that!
I'll put this
OUT OF ORDER
sign on the
merry-go-round."

"What a pity," said Dumbo. "The children won't have any fun tonight."

"Worse than that," said Mr. Donk, "I'm almost out of money. This is how I make my living. If the merry-go-round doesn't work, how will I survive? At one time, I could have cranked the motor by hand. But I'm too old now."

Dumbo smiled. "Don't be upset. Just take it easy. Timothy and I will look after the merry-go-round for you. I'll turn the crank with my trunk, and Timothy will collect the money from the children."

That's exactly what they did. That night, instead of working at the circus, Dumbo and Timothy stayed at the carnival making everyone happy. They made enough money to get the merry-go-round fixed.

Bongo Takes a Trip

One day Bongo the bear asked Lulubelle to go with him to Lake Aquarius for a picnic. The circus was closed for the day, so Bongo told her to meet him at the railroad station. She agreed, reminding him to be on time. "The train won't wait for anybody," she said.

"Don't worry," Bongo replied. "I'll be at the station."

He washed his face and oiled his one-wheel cycle, and soon he was whizzing down the road toward the station. He had just enough time to catch the train if he hurried. "Maybe I'd better take a short cut to make sure," he thought.

He went across a field and pedaled through some woods, dodging around the trees. "Taking a short cut is lots more fun than staying on a dull old road," he said to himself.

The cycling bear zipped
down little gullies
and around big rocks.
He came to a stream,
but he didn't stop.
He caught sight
of an old crocodile
stretched from
one bank
to the other.

"What a perfect bridge," he thought, and pedaled across the crocodile's back, balancing perfectly on his wheel. "Pardon me, Mr. Croc," he laughed, "I hope that didn't tickle!"

He was thinking that he should get to the station in plenty of time, when he heard two quick toots of the train whistle and the clanging of the engine bell.

"Oh no," he said in panic. "The train can't be leaving already." He turned on an extra burst of speed.

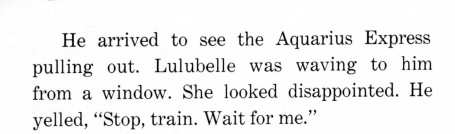

He arrived to see the Aquarius Express pulling out. Lulubelle was waving to him from a window. She looked disappointed. He yelled, "Stop, train. Wait for me."

As the engine kept chuffing down the track, Bongo was reminded of an old expression: "Time and tide and trains wait for no man or bear." He wasn't sure the quote was exact, but it was close enough. He had definitely missed his train!

Bongo stopped on the station platform to catch his breath. "Oh gosh," he sighed, "I guess my short cut wasn't short enough. What'll I do now?" He watched the train puff down the track toward the horizon. The engine seemed to say, "Chuff, chuff, chuff, you didn't go fast enough."

"Is that so?" exclaimed Bongo. "I'll show you I can go full steam, too." He took a deep breath, and down the platform he sped, churning the pedals of his cycle furiously. But following the train wasn't enough — he had to *beat* it to Lake Aquarius station.

"I never raced a train before," he thought. "It should be fun!"

Across the fields he went, and up and down the hills. The train had picked up lots of speed by now, and Bongo really had to make the pedals fly until they were just a blur!

He caught up with the train as it was puffing out the end of a tunnel. "Keep going, Mr. Engineer," he called. "I'll race you to the station." With that he zipped ahead and was out of sight over a hill before the rest of the train came out of the tunnel. He passed by farms and forests, streams and stands of magnificent evergreens, but Bongo didn't have time to enjoy all the beauty.

The little train pulled into the Lake Aquarius station and screeched to a stop. "All out for Lake Aquarius," shouted the conductor.

Lulubelle looked out of the train window, and there to her great surprise was Bongo!

They rented a canoe and glided over Lake Aquarius. She said, "I'm glad you made it, Bongo. I didn't expect to see you at the station."

"I said I'd be at the station, didn't I?" he answered. "But I didn't say which one!"

After the Hats

The Big Top was filled for the after-noon performance, and the animals and performers were lined up for the opening parade.

Suddenly a strong wind started whipping the tentflaps. The Big Top swayed and creaked, but there was no cause for concern — at least, not until one gust blew off Mr. Ringmaster's top hat.

SWOOOOSH!

"I hope he can catch it," said Dumbo.

The clowns laughed as Mr. Ringmaster raced after his hat. "He'll never catch up with that hat in a month of Tuesdays," they chuckled.

"We can't wait that long for the show to begin," Timothy Mouse said, "and we cannot start without Mr. Ringmaster. Come on, Dumbo. Let's get it back for him."

With a flap of his big ears, Dumbo flew after the top hat, and he grabbed it with his trunk.

As the elephant headed back to the Big Top, his own cap kept going straight ahead, carried by the strong wind. Timothy Mouse was in it!

"Help!" called Timothy. The mouse and Dumbo's cap sailed toward a nearby lake. Timothy was worried — he couldn't swim. He had only one chance and he took it. As the cap whizzed past some cattails, he reached out and grabbed one.

PLOP! Dumbo's hat splashed into the water, and Timothy clung to the swaying cattail yelling for help.

"Hang on," cried Dumbo. "I'll rescue you. Jump into Mr. Ringmaster's hat when I fly past."

The mouse jumped into the top hat. Next, Dumbo swooped low over the water, and Timothy reached down to get Dumbo's cap before it sank.

"Good," said Dumbo with a sigh of relief. "That was my favorite cap, and I didn't want to lose it."

"Well done, Dumbo," Mr. Ringmaster exclaimed when Dumbo gave him the top hat. "Now the show can begin. Stand by, everybody, and I'll lead the parade."

"But — but wait a minute," sputtered Dumbo. "You're walking off with Timothy and my cap."

Mr. Ringmaster didn't hear him. The band was playing a march, and the parade had begun. Dumbo fell into line with the other performers.

The parade circled the Big Top once, and Mr. Ringmaster stepped into the ring. The band stopped, and the crowd grew quiet.

Mr. Ringmaster shouted,
"Good afternoon,
ladies and gentlemen.
Welcome to the circus."

He took off his top hat and there, to everybody's surprise, was Dumbo's cap with Timothy sitting pretty as you please on Mr. Ringmaster's bald head.

The crowd roared with laughter.

"The more laughs the better at a circus," said Mr. Ringmaster. "Thank you, Dumbo. You've been a big help!"

Mickey and the Big Brown Bear

Mickey Mouse and Donald Duck were hiking through the woods one day, when Don stumbled on an empty soft drink bottle. "Waaaak!" he yelled.

"It's too bad people leave all these bottles and papers and wrappers and cartons. They make the woods ugly. Let's clean up the paths so other people won't get hurt," Mickey suggested.

"Clean up?" Donald shouted. "Not me! That's what I call *work*."

"Come on," Mickey laughed. "Maybe you can pick up another bottle before you trip on it."

"Absolutely not," Donald insisted.

Mickey got a big bag and began stuffing it with trash left by careless campers.

Donald saw a lumpy black thing under a bush. He wouldn't pick it up, but he stepped on it.

A terrifying roar filled the woods.

The black thing was attached to a giant bear. In fact, it was the bear's nose. Donald had tweaked the nose of a sleeping grizzly bear.

The bear raised up to his full height. "What are

you doing in my forest?" he asked.

"Er-ah, that is . . ." stammered Donald.

"You campers have not only cluttered up my home, you've disturbed my nap. Now get going!"

Donald took a long look at the huge figure looming overhead. In a flash he grabbed Mickey's bag and began stuffing it with trash. He stuffed and ran all the way back to the ranger station. When he arrived, the park was reasonably clean.

The bear winked at Mickey. "That's one way to get the old forest cleaned up, right?"

Mickey agreed.

"Let 'Em Eat Cake"

The circus was in town! With it came color and excitement, bands playing, clowns, people laughing and a big parade!

Who was leading the parade? Dumbo! He could walk, which he did on sunny days, and he could fly, which he did on rainy days (so he wouldn't get his feet wet). He was the star of the circus. His co-star was Timothy Mouse, who rode in Dumbo's hat.

Dumbo had been a circus star since he first flapped his big ears and realized he could fly. Each afternoon and evening he did power dives and outside loops inside the Big Top. He also flew to have fun or to help people.

He was leading the parade one day when suddenly he smelled something. Sniff! Sniff! Was it smoke? Timothy smelled it and exclaimed, "Let's find out where it's coming from. Maybe somebody needs our help."

Dumbo left the parade and turned
down a side street. He spied smoke
coming from a bakery shop.

"I wonder if the baker's bread is burning," said Timothy. When they flew into the bakery, they were greeted by clouds of smoke and wails of woe from Mr. Baker.

"Today I was going to bake some Christmas cookies," he said, "but the oven fire only makes smoke and won't burn. What am I going to do?"

Timothy, being smaller than Dumbo, hopped down to inspect the oven. He said, "I think Dumbo can fix it up. Come here, Dumbo. Bend down and get real close."

Mr. Baker thought maybe Dumbo would blow through his trunk to make the fire burn, but he never expected to see those two big ears begin flapping.

What a hurricane!

The wind blew away the clouds of smoke and made the fire light up. The blaze brightened the entire shop.

"Good job, Dumbo," cheered Timothy. "I knew you could do it."

"It's amazing," said Mr. Baker.

"You made the fire burn beautifully. Now I can begin baking my Christmas cookies."

Dumbo was happy when the smell of baking cookies replaced the smoke in the tiny shop. He started to leave, but Mr. Baker called him back. "You can't go yet. As soon as I finish frosting this big cake, I want you to have it as a thank you gift."

"I've got to go," said Dumbo. "Timothy and I are leading the circus parade, and we must hurry back."

Dumbo and Timothy rushed back to the parade and took their places in front. Mr. Ringmaster never even knew they were gone. When the parade was over, they played ball in the field near the circus. They were playing when they heard some shouting.

"Run for it!"

"Loose lion!"

Mr. Ringmaster raced by and hollered, "Look out, Dumbo. Look out, Timothy. The lion is loose. Run and hide."

Timothy looked at Dumbo and said, "Do you think we should run?"

"I should say not," Dumbo replied.

Sally and two of her seals passed by. "Lenny the lion is loose. Aren't you going to run for safety?" she called.

Dumbo answered, "No. We're having too much fun playing ball. Besides, we're not afraid of Lenny. He makes a lot of noise, but underneath he's all pussycat."

Timothy tossed the ball to Dumbo, who took a big swipe at it. CRACK! Dumbo whacked the ball. It took off like a rocket and clobbered Lenny the lion on his big nose.

Lenny had never been hit on the nose before, and he didn't like it one bit!

That ball stung
worse than
a swarm of bees!
Lenny rubbed
his tender nose
and yowled.
He charged
straight for Dumbo.

Dumbo saw the angry look in Lenny's eyes and knew the lion was a pussycat no longer! "Hop in my hat, Timothy," Dumbo said, and he soared into the air. Lenny tried to snap at the elephant, but Dumbo was too quick!

Dumbo flew to the acrobats' springboard, and Lenny was close behind. Lenny leaped, and Dumbo flapped his ears. The elephant glided away, but Lenny did a rolling belly flop into the sawdust pit.

Now Lenny was really mad.

Dumbo flew to the clowns' make-believe fire truck. He hovered behind the ladder. Lenny jumped and caught his neck in the rungs. He pulled free and fell. Steam spouted from the motor and took the curl out of Lenny's mane. Lenny was one beat-up lion.

Lenny bellowed and lunged for Dumbo, but he ended up in a tangle of fire hose.

Finally Dumbo flew toward the lion's cage. Lenny was close behind him. Dumbo cried, "Hold on tight, Timothy. I'll try to get him back in the cage."

Lenny followed Dumbo. He tried to slow down when he got inside the cage, but he was running full tilt and crunched into the iron bars.

CLUNK! Lenny flopped to the floor, his head spinning.

Dumbo flew outside the cage, and Timothy jumped down from Dumbo's hat and slammed shut the cage. Mr. Ringmaster ran up and locked the door. "Good for you, Dumbo," he panted.

Everybody congratulated Dumbo.

At that moment
Mr. Baker arrived
with a big cake.
He cut into it
and proclaimed:
"As I said before,
'Let 'em eat cake.' "

Bongo's Good Deed

One sunny afternoon Bongo was pedaling down the road. Suddenly a car sped past. Bongo saw that the rope holding the bags onto the car had broken. Everything was starting to wobble.

Bongo shouted, "Hey, something's wrong!"

The car was too far away, and nobody heard Bongo calling.

Bongo knew he couldn't catch up with the car because the road was steep and curvy as it circled a large hill. However, he knew he could take a short cut by crossing a river on some stepping stones. He began pedaling his unicycle toward the river.

As Bongo hurried
down the bank
on his cycle,
a friendly frog
croaked, "This way."
Bongo steered
toward the frog.

The frog continued, "Bounce from stone
to stone the way I do." He hopped up and
down as he talked.

Bongo bounced from one stone to the next. "This is fun," he cried. "Wheee!" However, he pedaled very carefully — he didn't want to miss a stone and have the river sweep him away.

On the far side, the frog waved a green goodbye to Bongo as the bear made his way up the path toward the road. He arrived just as the car roared by.

At that moment the rope broke, and the toys and bags started to fall off.

A big red ball
bounced off the car
and onto the pavement.

Bongo let the ball
bounce once,
and then he caught it.
"Gotcha!" he cried.
A bucket slipped off.
Bongo pedaled quickly
and caught it.
A picnic basket fell.
Bongo tried to catch it,
but he didn't have
three hands!

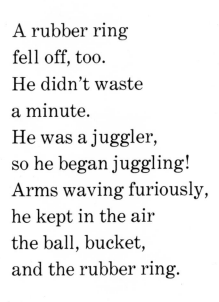

A rubber ring
fell off, too.
He didn't waste
a minute.
He was a juggler,
so he began juggling!
Arms waving furiously,
he kept in the air
the ball, bucket,
and the rubber ring.

By this time the people in the car realized what was happening. They stopped the car, and the children ran out and stared at the juggling bear on the unicycle. They began to applaud.

"Cut the applause," Bongo shouted, "and help me unload some of this stuff!"

The bear handed over the ball and the bucket and all the things that fell off the car. Not one item dropped — it was a perfect performance.

The children and their mother and father were so happy with Bongo that they invited him to share their picnic lunch. They spread a blanket near the river and put out all sorts of goodies.

"We can't thank you enough for your good deed," they said.

"Think nothing of it," said Bongo happily. "Juggling is fun for a bear like me, and you all know how much we bears enjoy a good picnic lunch."

They also saved some goodies for the friendly frog!

Pasting a Clown

Charlie the clown was very unhappy. Great tears dripped from his big, painted eyes and dribbled down his round nose. Dumbo and Timothy asked him what was wrong.

"The children don't think I'm funny anymore," Charlie explained. "No matter how hard I try, I can't make them laugh. I'm no good as a clown, so I'll have to leave the circus."

This made the little elephant and the mouse very sad. Mr. Ringmaster came along. He liked Charlie, too, and when he heard what was troubling the clown, he said, "Take a rest from being a clown. Go into town and paste up some circus posters. That would be helpful."

Charlie liked the idea of being helpful, and he felt happier.

Next morning Timothy and Dumbo found the paste pot and the brush hanging on a pole. "Charlie forgot his equipment," Timothy exclaimed.

"Charlie will never be able to put up the posters without paste and a brush, so we had better take them to him," the mouse added.

"We'll deliver them air express," said Dumbo, flapping his big ears. However, in their haste both Dumbo and Timothy forgot the paste brush.

They had no trouble finding Charlie. He was standing on a ladder, trying to hang a poster on a wall. The poster wouldn't stay up because there was no paste on it.

Charlie didn't think the project was very funny, and he was losing patience.

After Dumbo and the mouse arrived, Charlie laughed at himself. "No wonder the poster kept slipping down."

Then they both discovered that the brush had been left behind. "Oh, what a silly elephant I am," Dumbo sighed.

"Humph," Charlie humphed. "How can we brush on the paste without a brush?"

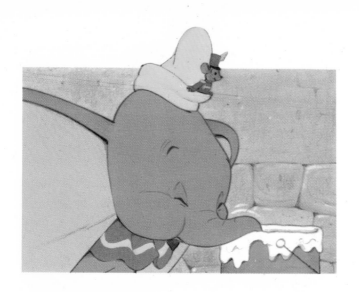

Little Timothy thought for a moment and came up with a good idea. "We can manage without a brush if Dumbo uses his trunk as a squirter," the mouse suggested. "He can squirt the paste on the wall, and Charlie can slap the poster into place."

They all agreed to Timothy's plan, and Dumbo began to fill his trunk with paste from the pot.

"YUCK!" sputtered Dumbo. "That stuff tastes terrible." He screwed up his face in disgust.

"Oooof," he said. "I've got to get rid of this awful stuff right away."

"Come on, Dumbo," Charlie called from the top step of the ladder. "Let me have the paste."

SWOOSH! PLOSH!

Charlie got it all right. Right in the back of the neck.

All the townspeople laughed and laughed.

Dumbo hadn't meant to shoot the paste at the clown, but he couldn't hold it in his trunk any longer. The little elephant looked at his friend all covered with paste, and he was very upset.

"I'm sorry, Charlie," he said. "I really didn't mean to squirt you."

Charlie didn't mind at all. He looked at all the laughing people and was glad. "Look how everyone is laughing," he said. "That's all that matters to a clown."

Charlie was so delighted that he hurried back to the circus with Dumbo and Timothy. He asked the elephant to do the squirting act with him every night in the center ring. To make it even more fun, Mr. Ringmaster made a special paste for Dumbo that tasted like raspberry sherbet. Dumbo liked it, except the seeds kept getting in his teeth. But as Timothy said so often, "Dumbo, that's show biz."

Boys and Gulls

One day Dumbo and Timothy Mouse were walking along the cliffs. The sun was shining, and the deep blue ocean washed up on the beach. Dumbo looked down at the golden sand and clear water and said, "How beautiful it is here. It's so peaceful and quiet."

There was a sharp cry!
"Help! Help!"
a voice called.
Dumbo and Timothy
couldn't see
anything.
"Please! Help!"
The elephant
and the mouse
looked harder,
without success.
The voice called,
"I can't get up
and can't get down."

Timothy listened and figured out where the voice was coming from. "Somebody is trapped on the cliff below us," he said.

"Jump into my hat, Timothy. We'll fly down and see who's in trouble."

Dumbo flapped his ears, and they soared over the cliffs.

Dumbo was proud
of his flying skill.
He soared
and turned
and drifted
and glided
toward the beach.
Finally they found
a young boy
trapped on a ledge
by the nest
of a sea gull.
He couldn't climb
up or down.

The boy stared and could hardly believe
his eyes when he saw the baby elephant
hover close by him.

"Jump on Dumbo's back," Timothy
called to the boy. "Hang onto his collar,
and we'll rescue you."

The boy jumped safely onto Dumbo's back and hung on tightly. Dumbo flapped his ears once, twice, three times, and flew to the top of the cliff.

"Whew!" the boy exclaimed as he hopped to the ground. "Thank you. I don't know what would have happened to me if you hadn't come along when you did."

"It's a good thing we heard you yell," said Timothy. "And it's a good thing that Dumbo can fly."

"You saved my life," the boy said. "How can I repay you?"

Dumbo saw the leather bag slung over the boy's shoulder. He thought the lad might have a sandwich in the bag which he would be glad to share.

"What have you in there?" Dumbo asked the boy.

"Sea gull eggs," he answered. "I took them out of the nest."

"So that is why you were climbing on that ledge," Dumbo said thoughtfully. "Don't you know that birds get upset and sad when their eggs are taken?"

"I'd never thought about that," the boy admitted.

"If you want to repay me for helping you," Dumbo said, "let me take the eggs back, and promise you will never take a bird's eggs again."

The boy gave the eggs to Dumbo. "I promise," he said. Then the little elephant flew down to the ledge.

The mother and father sea gulls were staring at their empty nest. When Dumbo brought their eggs back, they clapped their wings with delight.

Later Dumbo returned to the ledge, and there were three baby birds in the nest. Dumbo was very happy to see them.

Mickey and the Chewed Shoes

Chew, chew! Munch, munch! Gnaw, gnaw!

Pluto was having a wonderful time chewing on a pair of Mickey's shoes.

When Mickey found his shoes torn to pieces, he was very angry. "You naughty dog, Pluto. What am I going to do with you?"

Mickey decided that Pluto was chewing shoes to work off extra energy. Mickey told his nephews, "If Pluto got more exercise, he'd be too tired to chew. This afternoon I'm going to take him on a long hike."

That afternoon Mickey put on some comfortable shoes and took Pluto for a walk. They started out down the sidewalk. When they reached the edge of town, they walked along the gravel road. Mickey then set off cross-country. He climbed over a stile, crossed a meadow and hiked along a logging road. He climbed up a rocky path to Lookout Mountain, followed a path through the woods and finally arrived back home.

By this time Mickey was so tired, he couldn't put one foot in front of the other. He told the nephews,

"Now Pluto will be too worn out to chew up any more shoes."

Mickey was right, Pluto flopped into his basket and fell asleep.

Mickey relaxed in his favorite chair and called to his nephews, "Hey, boys, pull off my shoes for me, will you?"

Morty and Ferdie rushed forward to help Mickey. Suddenly they broke out laughing.

"What's so funny?" Mickey asked.

"Your shoes," said Morty and Ferdie. "They look worse than the pair Pluto chewed up last night!"

Jungle Sports

Mowgli found an old automobile tire one day at the edge of the jungle. He got some rope, tied it to a stout tree branch and was having a fine time swinging back and forth.

King Louie ambled up. "Hi, Mowgli. You look like one of my monkeys swinging up there."

"Oh, I'm not really much of a swinger," Mowgli replied.

"You'd better believe it," Louie replied. "Monkeys can run and jump and climb—and swing—better than any other jungle animal. Which reminds me, tomorrow is our annual Jungle Gold Medal Sports Day."

Mowgli asked, "What are you going to do about Shere Khan? Last year he barged in and said hunting monkeys was the best sport of all."

King Louie grew serious. "You're right! We should find a sure-fire way to get rid of Old Stripes so he won't spoil our fun. Got any ideas?" Mowgli thought for a moment.

Mowgli whispered something to King Louie, who agreed it was one fine idea. "I'll get on it first thing in the morning," he promised.

The sun was peeking over the tree-tops when Louie found Shere Khan.

"Morning, Shere Khan," said Louie.

"What's good about it?" growled the tiger.

"Well, today is Jungle Sports Day, and that's always fun."

"Yes, it is," agreed the tiger. "Maybe I could have a contestant or two for lunch."

"Oh, Sports Day isn't for tigers. You're not agile enough," said King Louie.

"What do you mean?" said Shere Khan.
"You can run okay, but can you jump?"
"Of course I can jump, you bunglehead!"
King Louie said slyly, "Then prove it by
jumping through that old tire."

Shere Khan said,
"That's easy."
He leaped.
THWUP!
Halfway through
he got stuck.
He thrashed
and howled
to no avail.

The jungle animals had their Sports Day, and through it all Shere Khan dangled helplessly, stuck in the tire. And Mowgli said, "Maybe by nightfall you'll be skinny enough to go all the way through!"

It's Done with Mirrors

Dumbo was sitting outside the circus tent enjoying the warm sunlight when Timothy Mouse dashed up. "Quick, Dumbo. Horatio the lion has escaped from his cage and can't be found."

"I wish we had stronger locks on the cages," said Dumbo. "First Lenny the lion gets loose, now Horatio. Who's next?"

Timothy squeaked,
"Horatio is
the biggest
and grumpiest
lion we've got.
If we run into him
we won't need
to worry about
who's next!"

Dumbo knew Timothy was right. He didn't like the idea of being on the ground with Horatio on the prowl. He told Timothy, "Since Horatio can't fly and I can, hop onto my cap and we'll get in some air time. We'll not only be safe up there, but maybe we can help find Horatio, too."

The elephant and the mouse took off and circled the tents.

They soared over the circus and looked closely at every shadow. "It's no use," Dumbo said at last. "I don't see Horatio anywhere."

"Maybe we'd better look for him on the ground. He might be hiding in one of the tents," Timothy suggested.

Fearfully Dumbo made a four-footed landing among the tents and skidded to a stop in front of the Hall of Mirrors.

"Don't forget," Timothy said, "Horatio doesn't get fierce unless someone steps on his tail."

Dumbo had never been in the Hall of Mirrors. With Timothy in his hat, he strolled inside.

"EEEeekk!" they both squealed when they found themselves facing a huge monster mouse!

What they saw was a reflection of Timothy in one of the funny-shaped mirrors that magnify. But Dumbo didn't know that.

"Let's get out of here!" he cried, racing to the exit.

As Dumbo was running from the tent, Horatio stalked by the entrance. Dumbo dashed out and didn't see the lion's tail in the doorway. THUMP! Dumbo's heavy foot landed smack on Horatio's tail.

"Oooaaarrhoo!" bellowed Horatio in angry surprise. "Get off my tail, leadfoot."

Dumbo gulped,
"Oh, excuse me."
The angry lion
glared at him.
"I'll teach you
to watch where
you put your
big flat feet!"

Timothy felt very brave. He leaned over the brim of Dumbo's hat and shouted, "You shouldn't be out of your cage, big mouth!"

That made Horatio
even more angry.
"Shut up, mouse,"
he raged.
"I'll stay out
of my cage
as long as
I want to."

"Then you'd better hide in that tent," Timothy said slyly, pointing to the Hall of Mirrors. "Your trainer is looking for you, and he isn't happy about your being free."

"Hmmm," growled Horatio. "Maybe you're right."

The lion hurried into the tent and promptly let out a bone-tingling roar of fear.

"Lion! Biggest lion in the world! He'll eat me up! Let me out of here!" Horatio roared.

Dumbo peeked around the corner. Horatio was looking at his reflection in the magnifying mirror and was scared to death!

"Yipes! Back to the cage. Only safe place from a monster like that," yelled Horatio. With a great leap he jumped over Dumbo and into his cage. He covered his eyes with his paws and cried, "Don't let that monster get me!"

The circus helpers arrived in time to lock the cage and applaud Dumbo and Timothy.

Mr. Ringmaster said, "Dumbo, you captured Horatio and taught him a trick. He'll now be known as a leaping lion!"

Bone Burying

Pluto was burying a bone.

The trouble was, he had picked the wrong place to bury it. The bone was going in the middle of Mickey Mouse's flower bed.

When he saw the earth and flowers flying in all directions, Mickey shouted, "Pluto, you know better than that! I'm working hard getting those flowers to grow. Take your bone and bury it someplace else. Bury it in a bed that doesn't have flowers in it."

Pluto walked around the garden with the bone in his mouth. He looked at all the different flower beds, and every one had seedlings growing in it. Pluto thought to himself, "If I start burying my bone in those beds, Mickey will say they are full of bulbs for the spring or summer."

Pluto walked on until he found another bed. This was full of cactus plants. He thought, "If I bury a bone there, I will end up with a nose full of stickers."

Pluto found a rock garden. He thought to himself, "I'll wear my paws to the bone trying to get at one grain of dirt."

Then Pluto had an idea. He knew exactly where he would bury his bone!

That night Mickey Mouse was very tired. He had been working hard in the garden all day, and he wanted to go to sleep. As he climbed between the sheets he leaped in the air. There was something cold in his bed. He reached down and got Pluto's bone.

He started to call Pluto and bawl him out, then he remembered that Pluto had done exactly what Mickey had told him.

Pluto had buried his bone in the only bed without any flowers in it!

The Train in Spain

Dumbo was a flying elephant, and he spent lots of time in the air. As a result, he didn't think much of jets or airplanes or balloons — they were nothing new to him. He preferred things that stayed on the ground. He liked hay rides, ferry boats and, best of all, trains. It made no difference if it were diesel, steam or electric — if it went on tracks, Dumbo wanted to ride it.

When the circus set up tents near the town of New Spain, Dumbo quickly learned that there was a miniature railroad nearby.

The first chance he got, Dumbo wanted to ride on the train. The opportunity came late one afternoon, after he had finished his act in the circus. He and Timothy Mouse hurried to the tiny station, and as they approached they heard a whistle blow and saw the engineer wave his flag.

Timothy said, "Get a move on, Dumbo, or we'll miss the train."

"I'm hurrying as fast as I can," Dumbo replied.

The two friends joined the happy children on the train. They scrambled into the caboose and began the ride.

They were going along happily, when suddenly there was a long hiss and the train stopped. The engineer jumped from the cab to see what was the matter. Timothy and Dumbo wondered what was wrong. On a railroad, a whole ride is fine, but half a ride is not very good.

The children were disappointed, so Dumbo and Timothy decided to see if they could help. They got out and walked toward the engineer. "What's the matter?" Dumbo called.

"Oh my," sighed the engineer. "The boiler is out of water."

"How could that happen?" asked Dumbo.

"I must have been pulling an extra-heavy load. Little children don't weigh much, but . . ." He looked at Dumbo. "By any chance were you riding on the train?"

"Yes," Dumbo replied.

"Well, that did it!" replied the engineer. "This train wasn't made to handle elephants! No wonder we ran out of water."

Dumbo felt very embarrassed.

"What can I do?"
Dumbo asked.
"The water tower
is clear back
by the station,"
the engineer
explained sadly.

Dumbo said, "I understand that the rain in Spain stays mainly on the plain, but I don't see any water around here. There isn't a lake or a river or a brook or anything. It looks like in New Spain only the *train* stays on the plain." Dumbo tried to make a joke, but the engineer didn't think it was funny.

"We need somebody to go to the water tower and bring the water back," he said. "If there were a taxi around here, or a bus, I could take them. But there isn't, and I'm too old to walk."

Dumbo knew *he* didn't need a taxi or a bus to get to the water. After all, he was a flying elephant; and since his weight had made the train run out of water, he felt that *he* should be the one to fix things.

"Leave it to me," he told the engineer. Timothy jumped in Dumbo's hat, Dumbo flapped his ears, and together the two of them flew to the water tower.

"Isn't it lucky I've got a trunk as well as these big ears?" Dumbo chuckled, popping his trunk into the tank of water.

He sucked up as much water
as he could, and then Dumbo
flew back to the train. All that
water made flying difficult,
but he soon hovered over the
engine and squirted water into
the thirsty boiler.

When Dumbo finished he got
into the caboose once more.

"Now we'll be off again," said
the engineer.

"Hooray!" cheered the children happily.

The engineer led a special "Hooray" for Dumbo, and he started the engine. The children enjoyed the ride so much they all bought tickets for another trip. Dumbo stayed in the caboose all afternoon. In fact, he rode the railroad so much that it became known as "Dumbo's Railroad."

Whenever Dumbo rode the train, the engineer was careful to keep plenty of water in the boiler. He knew that the rain in New Spain

didn't stay in the train — it stayed in the water tank, except when Dumbo was along to help out.

Up, Up and Away

One day Dumbo went for a walk in town. As usual, Timothy rode on the brim of his hat. They saw their friend Albert, who was selling balloons on the sidewalk. Albert was very hungry — it was late afternoon and he hadn't had lunch yet — but he didn't know what to do with his balloons while he ate. Then along came a little boy.

"Little boy," said Albert, "if you will hold my balloons while I go for a hamburger, I will give you a free balloon."

"Fine," agreed the boy.

So Albert handed him the balloons and dashed off to buy a hamburger with lots of onions and a pickle on top.

Unfortunately the little boy didn't weigh as much as Albert, and the balloons floated him off the ground. Up, up, up he went.

"Help!" the boy shouted. "I'm being kidnapped by a bunch of balloons."

Luckily Dumbo and Timothy saw what was happening. "We must rescue the little boy," Timothy said, pointing upward.

"If we don't
save him,
he won't be able
to go to school
tomorrow.
Imagine how sad
he will be!"

Dumbo wasn't sure if the boy would be
sorry to miss school, but he agreed that the
lad needed saving. The elephant waggled his
ears, and a moment later he was flying.

By now the little boy was sailing high over the rooftops of the town. "Help, or I'll be late for supper," he cried.

"I knew he wouldn't be worried about missing school tomorrow," Dumbo said to himself as he glided toward the boy.

Timothy squeaked instructions. "Sit on Dumbo's back and hold on tight."

The boy settled on Dumbo's spine, holding onto the elephant's collar with one hand and clutching the balloons with the other.

"Down we go!" yelled Dumbo, doing a loop-the-loop.

While the boy was riding in the sky with Dumbo, Albert had finished his lunch and returned to the street corner. He looked everywhere for the boy and the balloons, but they were gone.

Albert heard
flapping noises
in the sky.
He looked up.
"My word," he said.
"I'm seeing things.
It must have been the
extra pickle I ate for lunch!"

Dumbo came to a landing on the sidewalk, filing his toe nails on the cement as he skidded to a stop in front of Albert. The boy hopped off Dumbo's back and returned the balloons.

"Thanks for helping me out," said Albert. "Here are two balloons for taking such good care of them."

The boy ran all the way home so he wouldn't be late for supper.

The Great Ravioli

One day a new performer joined the circus. His name was The Great Ravioli. Neither Dumbo nor any of the other circus people had ever heard of him before he arrived, but afterward they heard about him all the time. The Great Ravioli always talked about himself. The air around the circus was heavy with his bragging and boasting.

"You are so lucky," The Great Ravioli kept telling everybody, "because The Great Ravioli is now the star of your circus."

Dumbo said to Timothy Mouse, "I wish he wouldn't keep telling us how wonderful he is. All he does is brag, brag, brag."

They watched
The Great Ravioli
practice his act.
The Great Ravioli
did flips
to the front
and flips
to the back.
He did spins,
and he twirled
upside down.
The Great Ravioli
was a talented
performer.

"I wish I could do stunts like that," Dumbo sighed.

"Why not try?" Timothy suggested.

"Okay, why not?" Dumbo answered.

When The Great Ravioli had finished, Dumbo stood on the end of the big seesaw and Timothy Mouse prepared to jump on the other end.

"All set?" asked Dumbo.

"Let's go!" cried Timothy.

They were interrupted by gales of loud laughter. "Ho, ho, ho. That teeny-weeny mouse will never send you into the air! He's too small. You need someone heavier. Even I, The Great Ravioli, great as I am, could not send an elephant into the air." He danced away, laughing.

The Great Ravioli was right. Timothy jumped as hard as he could on the plank; but the other end of it, where Dumbo was sitting, didn't move.

Timothy tried again. Nothing.

The elephant and the mouse began to feel very silly. All day long they heard The Great Ravioli's unkind laughter. Finally Dumbo had an idea, and he talked to Mr. Ringmaster about it. They agreed that Dumbo could teach The Great Ravioli a lesson.

That evening all the seats were filled, and everybody clapped when The Great Ravioli was introduced. His act was a big success, and his spins and twirls and jumps delighted the audience.

When he finished, Dumbo and Timothy entered the ring. The spotlight washed them with warm white light.

The Great Ravioli asked Mr. Ringmaster, "What's going on?"

"Dumbo's going to try an act like yours," answered Mr. Ringmaster.

The Great Ravioli smiled — he knew Dumbo would make a fool of himself.

This time, when Timothy jumped on one end of the seesaw, Dumbo flapped his ears and soared into the air. The audience cheered. All the circus people were happy, too. "You've shown The Great Ravioli you're smarter than he is!" they said.

As for The Great Ravioli, he never bragged or boasted again.

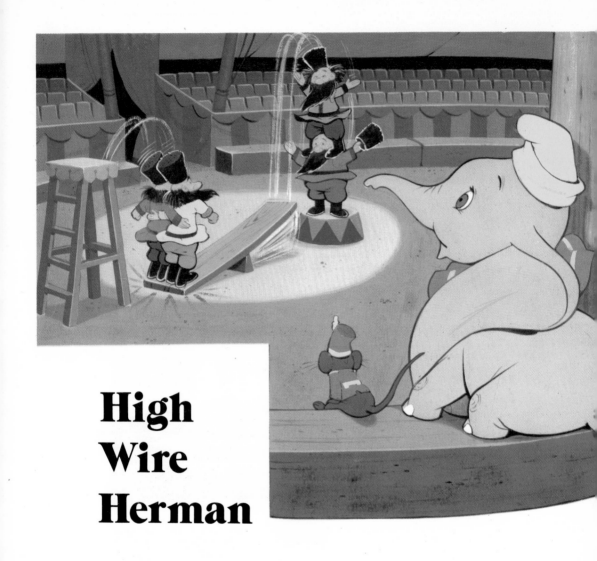

High
Wire
Herman

Dumbo and Timothy Mouse were watching the Russian acrobats practice their act. Two acrobats jumped on one end of a springboard, and their friend on the other end bounced high in the air.

Timothy said, "I'd like to try it, Dumbo, if you promise to catch me."

After the acrobats had left, Timothy dashed out to the springboard. Dumbo climbed on the stand.

Dumbo yelled, "Here goes!"

He jumped *down* on his end of the spring-board, and Timothy shot *up*.

Dumbo weighed more than the acrobats, and the mouse weighed less. As a result, Timothy went up, *up*, UP! "I think I'm practically in orbit!" he shouted. "Whee! Look at me!"

Suddenly Timothy
began to worry
that he might never
come down.
What could he do?

He spied the wire used by High Wire Herman. Grabbing it and holding on tight, he cried out, "Help!"

It was a good thing the mouse yelled, because High Wire Herman had begun to practice. He was walking on his wire, balancing himself with an umbrella, and he stopped just in time.

Herman saw the mouse
clutching the wire.
"Why, I nearly
stepped on you,"
Herman said.
"I'm glad you didn't,"
Timothy replied.
"Can you get me down?
I'm feeling dizzy."

"Hang on," Herman urged, looking down. "Help is on the way."

Dumbo was waggling his ears and flying to the rescue. He held his cap in his trunk and called to the mouse, "Hop in the hat."

The mouse was safe at last.

They apologized
to Herman
for upsetting
his practice.
"Don't worry,"
he answered.
"I need company.
It's lonely
on that wire."

That night Dumbo and Timothy remembered
what Herman had said about being lonely.
They flew to his platform to keep him company.

"Why, it's a
wonderful view,"
said Dumbo.
"What a fine seat
for a circus!"

Dumbo Helps Out

Though Dumbo worked in the circus, he often enjoyed getting away from the Big Top. He liked to explore each of the towns where the circus stayed. Because he made friends easily, he talked and visited with townspeople everywhere.

And he was often able to help them.

One day, for example, he and Timothy Mouse were walking down the main street of Centerville, looking in store windows and watching the children in the park.

At a street corner they saw a little girl crying. "Oh — sob — I left my dolly on the bus."

Her mother said, "Susie, I told you not to bring your doll."

"I thought my doll would like to visit downtown. She gets so lonesome by herself in my room," replied the girl. "Besides, she really enjoyed the movie last week."

Dumbo felt sorry for little Susie.

"Dry your tears, Susie.
I'll get your doll back,"
Dumbo told her.
She clapped her hands in glee.

She said, "Why, it's Dumbo. From the circus. I know all about you, Dumbo. If anybody can get my doll back, you can."

Dumbo flapped his ears and flew down the street.

Dumbo could fly fast when he had to, so he zoomed after the bus. Little Timothy held on tightly to Dumbo's hat. Soon they were out in the country, following the bus.

When the bus came to the next stop, Dumbo and Timothy were waiting for it. The conductor had found Susie's doll, and he was holding it in his hand.

"I've come
for the doll.
May I have it?"
asked Dumbo politely.

The conductor
hated circuses,
so he didn't know
about Dumbo.
He was shook up
to see
a baby elephant
asking for a doll.
He panicked.

"Great galloping goats!" he gasped. He dropped the doll, jumped back in the bus and drove away. He was so upset he missed two stops completely and carried three members of the Hoganville String Quartet to the wrong town!

Dumbo picked up the doll and flew back to Susie. Her mother was very surprised, but Susie explained to her mother how smart Dumbo was.

The mother was so impressed with Dumbo that she promised to take Susie to that night's performance. What more could a circus elephant ask?

As the circus moved from one location to another, Dumbo was always helpful.

He captured three bank robbers who had disguised themselves as window washers and were hiding out on the forty-fourth floor of the Seegrin Building. Only Dumbo was able to fly up and get close enough so that Timothy could slip on the handcuffs.

He found three missing boys who had gone fishing in the town water tower and were unable to get down. Dumbo delivered them safe and sound to their mothers.

When Joe Claptrap's poodle vanished, Dumbo tracked her to the Sweete Doggie Beauty Salon, where she was being made over into a collie.

By this time it was winter. Though Dumbo enjoyed flying in the cold air, he often thought about sledding.

Dumbo told Timothy, "I sure would like to slide down a hill on a toboggan."

The little elephant flew to the foot of a hill for a closer look at the sledders. After he landed, however, he was more interested in one boy who wasn't having fun like the other children. On his sled was a big shopping basket, and he was trying to haul it up the hill.

"He needs some help," Dumbo said.

Then the sled collapsed.

CRRAASH!

The basket of groceries fell into the snow. Cans, packages, boxes and all sorts of things

were scattered all over. The boy didn't know what to do.

"Don't worry," said Dumbo. "We'll have these things back in your basket in two shakes of an elephant's tail."

"But how can I get Mom's groceries home now?" he asked.

"We live on the top of the hill, and the basket is too big for me to carry."

"We'll *fly* home. It's sort of your own personal air mail," said Timothy.

They picked up the boxes and cans and cartons, and Dumbo said to the boy, "Have you ever ridden a flying elephant?"

"I've never ridden any kind of elephant," the boy answered.

"Then hop on." Flapping his ears, Dumbo took off and went flying up the hill like a fat jet.

The other boys and girls laughed. "Hooray for Dumbo," they cried, waving their arms. "He's pretending to be a flying taxicab. What fun!"

Dumbo landed in the boy's yard. "Door-to-door service — almost," he smiled.

The boy called to his mother, "I'm home."

The boy's mother thanked Dumbo for helping out. She said, "It must be exciting to fly."

"What really sounds exciting is going sledding," Dumbo replied. The boy let Dumbo and Timothy use his new toboggan.

So Dumbo and Timothy played with the boys and girls. Next season he knew he would have good friends waiting in every town. He was not only a flying elephant, but the best-loved elephant in the world.